-Louise M.
Miller

Magic Charms:
The Kangaroo Kraze

Book Two

by LOUISE MARIE MILLER

ISBN 978-1-387-65652-3

Photographs by Pat Schumacher

Printed and bound in the U.S.A.

First Edition April 2018

www.lulu.com/spotlight/louisemariemiller

This book is dedicated to my mom, dad, and younger sister, Vivian, for showing me support and loads of encouragement throughout my entire life.

CONTENTS

FOREWORD

Several years ago I had the pleasure of meeting Louise Miller as I assembled some magical trees in her living room in honor of her 8th birthday party which was themed after the movie *Maleficent*. Louise also admires Princess Merida from *Brave* for obvious reasons... she has glorious red hair like Louise and is a girl who is daring, brave, and always stands up for what she believes in.

In the summer of 2017, I discovered that Louise wrote a book and had it published! As a Library Media Specialist in a neighboring school district, I was so very impressed with her imagination, determination, and perseverance to take on such a task from beginning to end at the age of 10!

On her 11th birthday, I invited her to be a guest author at a school where I am the Library Media Specialist. Louise made her first public appearance. She stood in front of approximately 200 children, teachers, and administrators and presented her background through a PowerPoint presentation that allowed all of the children to make a connection with her. Louise spoke of her family, playing soccer, running races, traveling, watching movies, creating movies, doing art activities, Lego building and more. She spoke about her inspiration for writing the book, how she developed the characters, the time she dedicated to it, and she read a few pages aloud. She continued with many school visits after that... all successful!

The young minds of the school audiences Louise spoke to could find inspiration and make connections with this budding young author. Needless to say, *Magic Charms: The Adventure Begins* by

FOREWORD

Louise Miller, has been checked out of our Library over and over. All of the students are hoping for more books by this amazing young author. Louise Miller is a vibrant young lady with a brilliant future who can inspire all students she meets and adults alike.

Cindy Rizzolino

February 2018

Magic Charms:
The Kangaroo Kraze

Book Two

Chapter One

Surprise Visit

"Over here, Maria!" shouted Kasandra, as her older sister passed her the soccer ball.

"Anytime!" shouted back Maria, as Kasandra received the ball. Kasandra was going to try out for the MaryEllen Bay Middle School soccer team. Soccer was something she played in her free time. She used to play it all the time with Maria in Brazil. Now, she plays with Maria in the United States of America. A few months ago, Kasandra's family moved from Brazil to Hartford, Connecticut.

"Girls! Time to come in for dinner!" said Kasandra's mother, who was walking through the open doorway.

"Coming, Mom!" said Kasandra, as she ran into the kitchen of her grand American home. Tonight was her favorite night of the week. It was Tuesday. Not only was it on a Tuesday that Kasandra's family moved to America, but today was also Taco Tuesday. Mom made the girls try multiple new foods every week. The family loved

Mom's tacos so much that every Tuesday turned into "Taco Tuesday." Maria said that tacos were something they had every week in the high school. *Tacos twice a week? I can't wait to go to the high school!* thought Kasandra the first time they had Taco Tuesday at home.

Mom set the taco supplies on the table so everyone could assemble their own tacos. "Where's Dad?" asked Kasandra out of curiosity.

Mom frowned. "He had to work late at AT&T. He won't be here for dinner tonight. He might not be here 'til you two are in bed. I'm sorry, honey."

"It's okay," replied Kasandra, as she took a tortilla off one of Mom's blue plates.

Dad always made the entire family laugh during dinner. Once when Mom made spaghetti and meatballs, Dad took some uncooked noodles and put two in his nose. He made his nose twitch like a rabbit. He called the trick "The Golden Noodle." It made everyone laugh, even Mom.

Mom was big on spending lots of time with her family. She worked as an elementary school speech therapist and made a point to never have out-of-school meetings. Mom was also sure to be ready for work early enough each morning to drive Kasandra to school. Mom had started driving her more often after Kasandra nearly got hit by a delivery truck one morning when she was walking to school. Luckily, she jumped out of the way just in time. Since then, Kasandra and her mom made sure that she almost never had to walk to school anymore.

The girls loaded up their tacos and started to eat. Kasandra put lettuce, cheese, taco meat, tomatoes, and sour cream on hers. It was really good! Kasandra called it "The Everything." She called it that because it literally had everything Mom set out for them to use in it. Kasandra definitely got the name making trait from her dad.

When they finished their tacos, Kasandra and Maria settled in to start an episode of *Daredevil*. *Daredevil* was Kasandra's favorite superhero. He was left blind after a boyhood accident. Now he's a superhero who fights crime at night. *He's pretty cool. I wish I was as much of a superhero as Daredevil,* Kasandra thought to herself as the girls watched the show. After the episode was over, Kasandra went upstairs to put on her pajamas. The first pajamas Kasandra grabbed were her pink monkey PJs. They were a little small for her, but they were in decent shape, other than a few grass and dirt stains.

It was only six PM, so Kasandra had plenty of spare time to read before bed. She grabbed *The Girl Who Drank The Moon* off her shelf, sat down on her bed, and began reading. After a half an hour of reading, the doorbell rang. Kasandra jumped up, but then heard Maria shout, "I got it!" With that, Maria opened the door and said, "Kasandra, it's for you."

Kasandra jumped. No one ever showed up for her at this time of day. Maybe her friends would come over after school, but not any time after dinner. The thought of someone coming to her house made

Kasandra think, *Oh my, I need to change out of these pajamas! There might not be much of a chance that George Clooney is knocking on my front door, but there is still a chance!* She quickly changed into a t-shirt, shorts, and sandals. She dashed into the bathroom, grabbed a hair tie, and pulled her black hair into a bun. Then she left.

Kasandra ran down the carpet covered stairs and walked over to the living room. There, sitting on one of the couches was the one and only, John Martin. John was one of the people Kasandra had met in school a few months ago. He was also Kasandra's first American crush. She kept looking. Next to John was Shakira Umbridge. On the couch across from John and Shakira sat Darling Adams. Darling was a kind girl who happened to be blind, and was a very good friend. Shakira was, well, Kasandra's best friend. The others came in a close second though.

"Hey, Kasandra!" said Darling, as she waved Kasandra over to the couch. Kasandra sat down, waiting to hear what her friends were there to say.

"So, we want to talk about the Animal Guard," started John. "We've been thinking..." he continued.

"That maybe we need code names!" finished Shakira.

"Hey! I was gonna say that!" exclaimed John.

The Animal Guard was a secret organization they had been recruited to a few months ago. They have been assigned to travel the globe together to save animals and their habitats from all sorts of

dangers. The biggest danger of them all being Crow and \
former members of the Animal Guard who had gone rogue.

Shakira smiled proudly at their idea.

"So, what do you think?" asked Darling calmly.

"I love it!" replied Kasandra. *What a good idea!* she thought silently. "Do we get to pick them?" she asked curiously.

"Yep," replied Shakira quickly. She was still smiling ear-to-ear.

"So, what's it gonna be, Kasandra?" asked John.

"This is hard." Kasandra tapped her chin deep in thought. "Ooh! How about 'Kitty?' That's what my older sister Maria calls me in our secret codes we like to make up. What do you think?"

"I love it!" exclaimed Darling and Shakira at the same time. The two girls burst out laughing. Kasandra and John couldn't help but laugh too.

"So 'Kitty' it is then," said Shakira. "So, what's mine?"

"Hmmm," said Darling. "How about 'Peacock Princess?'"

"I'm satisfied with that," replied Shakira.

"John's next!" said Kasandra.

"Oh, no," said John, looking concerned.

Then Shakira suggested, "I like 'The Parrot.' How do you feel about that, John? It kinda makes you sound intimidating."

"I like that. John, Awesomeness, Hope, and The Parrot God!" said John before the entire room burst into tears from laughing too much!

"Alright, enough with the speech, parrot boy," said Shakira to John.

"It's 'The Parrot' to you, loyal servant," replied John with a laugh.

"Good luck with that," said Shakira, officially ending the argument.

"Well, well, well. Darling still needs a code name," Kasandra pointed out to the rest of the group.

"What's it going to be?" asked Darling politely.

"How is 'Darling Deer?'" asked John.

Shakira interrupted, "I don't think it's safe to say our real names in the code names. It could expose who we are to Crow and Vulture."

"Oh," replied John.

"Well, Darling did go really fast and was very brave in that zebra mission. That makes her pretty daring," commented Shakira.

Kasandra thought for a moment. "How about 'Daring Deer?'"

"You're a genius!" said Darling, once again politely.

"Why, thank you," replied Kasandra, faking a British accent. She pretended to drink invisible tea with her pinky finger raised daintily in the air. Darling joined the pretend tea party too.

"I think Maria has the phone. Maybe you could call your parents and see if you can sleepover," suggested Kasandra hopefully.

"Sorry, Kasandra. I can't. My Dad has a business meeting tonight. Plus, I promised my Mom I would watch Food Network with her," said Shakira.

"I can't either. Julia and Jeremiah need babysitting early tomorrow," Darling said with a frown.

"I could, but I promised my neighbor that I would help fix his bike first thing in the morning," said John at last.

"Oh. It's okay," said Kasandra. "Maybe another night."

Chapter Two

The One and Only Jessica

The next morning, Kasandra got dressed, ate breakfast, brushed her hair and teeth, then hopped into her mom's car. "Do you have everything?" asked Mom, as she buckled up her seat belt.

"I do. Don't worry, Mom. I got it under control," replied Kasandra.

"Oh, really?" said Mom, as she started the car. Kasandra and Mom giggled, and before they knew it, they were at MaryEllen Bay Middle School. The school wasn't far from their house, but Mom liked to drive Kasandra to school in the mornings. However, Kasandra preferred to walk home with her friends after school.

"Bye, Mom. See you later!" Kasandra hopped out of the car and waved to her Mom as she drove away from the school. Kasandra walked through the big doors with all of her classmates. She walked to her locker, unlocked it, removed the books she needed, and headed to Mrs. Brown's classroom for science.

Kasandra had been reading about so many different things in science like magnets, fungi, and plants. But today was special. Today they would get to pick lab partners for the year. Well, more like Mrs. Brown would get to pick them.

Kasandra hurried into the classroom after hearing the bell ring. Kasandra took her seat in the back of the room. She looked up at her science teacher and smiled, hoping she would get a good partner for the year. The teacher was wearing a black dress and black flats. To top it off, she had on a white lab coat and goggles on top of her head. She had soft skin and long pink hair. Her hair was tied into a ponytail, and her pink strands of hair moved swiftly behind her when she walked.

Kasandra could see that the teacher was holding a paper in her hands, also known as "The List." *The lab partners list.* Kasandra tried to get a quick glance at the piece of paper, but all she could see was a letter "J" closest to her own name. Kasandra started guessing who her partner would be. *Maybe my partner is John, or Janet, or it could be...*

Once the rest of the class arrived, Mrs. Brown started to announce lab partners for the year. Kasandra was at the end of the list. "Antonio and Darling. John and Shakira. Last, but certainly not least, Kasandra and Jessica." *Great. I'm stuck with Jessica as my lab partner. Gee, I wonder who will be doing all the work!* thought Kasandra. She sighed and went over to sit by Jessica, who refused to move from her own seat.

"You have the rest of the class period to find a way to turn a banana into a battery. If you need help, open your science book to page 173. Your time starts now," directed Mrs. Brown. Then she sat down in her chair.

Kasandra opened her book and started reading. "What do I even do in this class anyways?" said Jessica, as she started to twist her fingers in her blonde curls.

"Maybe you should do less fooling around and more working?" Kasandra replied to her.

Jessica's mother was the principal, Principal Morrison. Jessica never got in trouble. The word around school was that if she talked back to the teacher, she would tell her mom, and the teacher would be fired. Jessica didn't get in trouble, she *was* the trouble. Or the "drama mama," as Shakira liked to call her.

"Whatever," said Jessica. "Why are we even talking?"

"Because you asked a question, so I answered it." Kasandra turned away from Jessica and stuck a red wire into the banana.

Jessica quickly shot back, "Ugh! Just do the work, science nerd."

"Girls, less talking, more working," called Mrs. Brown from across the room.

"Yes, Mrs. Brown," replied Kasandra and Jessica at the same time. Jessica gave Kasandra a nasty look, then began playing with her hair again. Kasandra gave her a nasty look back.

Now, how do I turn a banana into a battery? Kasandra thought to herself, as she stuck a blue clip into the banana. *Only fifty-nine more minutes with Jessica.* Kasandra watched the clock as the seconds slowly ticked by.

When science class finally came to an end, Kasandra rushed out the door to meet her friends at their lockers.

"How are you after 'it' happened?" asked Shakira, as she grabbed her reading book.

"And to believe I was actually beginning to enjoy science class," replied Kasandra with a frown. "Until Jessica became my lab partner, that is."

Shakira smiled. "At least we're still reading buddies," she said. That brightened up Kasandra's mood. They heard the bell ring and headed down the hallway with the rest of the students.

After school, the gang walked back to Kasandra's house. They went straight upstairs to Kasandra's bedroom. They were going to work on some homework together. And talk.

"Shakira, how do you divide thirty-three thousand, four hundred and ninety by three?" John asked.

"Why would I tell you?" replied Shakira, whose vivid red hair was up in a ponytail.

"Because....."

"Admit it John, you don't know the answer," Shakira laughed, glancing over at Kasandra.

"So," began Kasandra, "I was thinking we could start doing more research. Ya know, on *La Guarda Animal.*"

"English, please?" said Shakira.

"Oh, yeah. Sorry, guys," replied Kasandra.

"It's okay," said Darling. Darling was wearing her typically straight, blonde hair in the most beautiful curls Kasandra had ever seen. They bounced gently each time Darling nodded her head.

They finished up their homework, hurried downstairs, and grabbed the fruit basket off the kitchen island. Then they raced back to Kasandra's room, grabbed a pen and paper, and rushed down the hall. The house had two hallways at the top of the stairs. There was the "East Hallway" and the "West Hallway," as Kasandra and Maria nicknamed them. The foursome took the East Hallway. They walked past several rooms, until they reached what they were looking for. At the end of the hallway was a door. *The door.* That is, the door to headquarters.

The group made this attic area their very own hideout. But they called it "headquarters" for Animal Guard purposes. They had gotten computers placed in the attic space to do their research. What research? They had to study different animals so they would know animals' fears, predators, and ways that they could help them. They were also researching Crow and Vulture, who liked to cause trouble all over the world.

The group's most recent mission was saving a baby zebra from a vicious hyena. Without a doubt, their mission had been a success.

"Let's do this," Kasandra said, as they all sat down and flicked on the computer. The group worked late into the night and soon drifted off to sleep.

Chapter Three

Free Kicks and Foul Shots

Today was the big day. Today was the MaryEllen Bay Middle School's soccer team tryouts. And Kasandra was going to try out for a position on the co-ed team. Kasandra loved soccer. Soccer was a big thing back in Brazil. With Pelé, the world's greatest soccer player of all time, being from Brazil, Kasandra knew a thing or two about the sport. Kasandra had brought with her to America all of her soccer gear.

Now Kasandra gently opened one of the dresser drawers in her bedroom. Inside the drawer was her soccer kit. She had soccer socks with pink and white stripes on them, and shin guards that matched. On top of it all were her soccer cleats. They were pink as well, with glittery laces, and on the side they said, "Viva Livre."

"Live Free," Kasandra muttered to herself, as she examined the cleats with admiration. The shoes still looked brand new, even though Kasandra had worn them many times before.

"Kasandra! It's time to go!" called Mom from the kitchen.

"Coming!" shouted Kasandra, as she shoved the cleats into her Nike gym bag. She ran into the kitchen, grabbed her lunch, and hurried out the front door to Mom's car. Kasandra was ready to take on the day!

The school day went by even slower than Kasandra thought it would. Seconds felt like minutes, minutes felt like hours, and hours felt like days. Finally the bell was about to ring, and that also meant the end of Mrs. Giamoni's history class. Only one question was left on her quiz.

How tall was Abraham Lincoln?
A. 6' 4"
B. Too Tall to Count
C. 5' 7"

Kasandra quickly circled the letter *A* right before the bell rang. A sigh of relief gushed out of her.

"Hey, hey. Settle down class," Mrs. Giamoni said. "It's not the first time that bell has rung." Today's outfit of Mrs. Giamoni's was a light pink pantsuit with dark gray heels. She reminded Kasandra of the character Dolores Umbridge in the *Harry Potter* books. All that pink. It was Kasandra's favorite color. Although purple had grown on her lately as well.

Kasandra grabbed her books and headed down the hallway to pack up her things. She saw her fellow students rushing down the hallway and to their buses. Kasandra started to make her way in the opposite direction of the crowd. Soon she reached the gymnasium. The gymnasium had large wooden bleachers and high ceilings. The floors shined so brightly that Kasandra could see her reflection in them. She saw the other students who were trying out for the soccer team, and made her way over to the bleachers to sit down next to Shakira.

"Yes! You made it!" said Shakira, as she hugged her bestie.

"I know! History almost bored me to death!" Kasandra said, trying to imitate Shakespeare. She couldn't help but let out a chuckle, and apparently neither could Shakira. Their laughter was interrupted by the sharp sound of a whistle. It was Coach Jim. All the chatter ended, and everyone had their eyes on the instructor.

"Listen up. I want all the boys on this side, and all the girls sitting on the bleachers. Are we clear?" he said in his sergeant-like voice.

The athletes promptly responded, "Yes, sir!" The boys quickly made their way over to the center of the gym and stood in a straight line.

"Start kicking and passing the ball. I will be over in a minute." The coach walked over to the girls. "Alright. Any cheerleaders, go to the right corner of the gymnasium. Any soccer players, follow me."

A large amount of girls walked over to the right corner of the gym, where they began practicing cartwheels and splits. Then, Kasandra recognized the shiny blonde hair of Jessica Morrison and her "blue" sense of fashion. Not only did she see Jessica, but next to her was Darling and about twelve other girls. All the girls were perfectly fit, their hair up in tight buns, wearing nothing but snug leotards and shorts that matched. Kasandra turned away and followed her coach towards the center of the gym.

"Line up behind the boys," said Coach Jim loudly. Kasandra followed the rest of the line and watched the others while she waited for her turn to kick the soccer ball.

When it was Shakira's turn, she nailed it right into the top left corner of the goal. "That was a very good shot, Shakira," Coach Jim commented, as he marked something down on the clipboard he had in front of him.

"Please, call me future *M.V.P.*," replied Shakira with a smirk.

"I'll see what I can do," said the coach, and he marked something down again on his clipboard. "Next!"

Now it was Kasandra's turn. It was all up to this one shot to make the team. She took one, then two, steps back, and took one step to the left. She ran and kicked the ball as hard as she could. It hit off her laces and soared right over the goalie's head. *Yes!* Kasandra silently cheered. She saw the coach's jaw drop.

"Very good job, Miss Cortez," said Coach Jim. He once again wrote something down on his clipboard.

"That shot was amazing, Kasandra!" squealed Shakira a little while later as the two girls walked to Shakira's mom's car.

"It wasn't as good as yours!" replied Kasandra happily.

"Come on, girls!" called Shakira's mother. The girls hopped into the car, and before they knew it they were at Kasandra's house. As she slipped out of the car, Kasandra thanked her friend's mom greatly and quickly ran into her blue colonial style house.

Kasandra settled herself at the kitchen island, took out her homework, and started on the math page she had in her workbook. She glanced over at her older sister Maria, who was sitting at the island working on homework as well, as her perfectly straight teeth sunk into an apple.

"How was your day, Kitty?" asked Maria, putting down the apple. Maria was perfect. Most people say you can't define perfect, but Maria *was* perfect. Her long silky black hair, with sparkling eyes, paired perfectly with her never-chapped lips.

"It was good," said Kasandra, flipping through the pages of her math workbook once more.

"So how was your soccer try-out?" asked Maria with much interest.

"It was great! And I scored!" replied Kasandra with a broad smile on her face. "I can't wait until Monday when we find out who made the team," she continued with glee.

"That's great!" replied Maria, as she picked up her phone and began texting someone.

"Who are you texting?" asked Kasandra, taking a grab for the phone.

"Hey!" said Maria, pulling the phone away from Kasandra. Kasandra continued to try to sneak the phone from Maria which forced Maria to stand up, raising the phone above her head, to keep it out of Kasandra's reach. Kasandra jumped for it and successfully grabbed the phone out of her older sister's hands. Kasandra ran. What else was she supposed to do? Phone in hand, she darted into the living room like a cheetah in high gear, running quickly up the stairs before landing swiftly on the couch back in the blue living room.

Maria thought that Kasandra went up to her bedroom with her phone, but she didn't. Before ending up in the living room, Kasandra had run to her room and climbed out of her bedroom window, jumping to the soft grass below and re-entering the house through the back door. Kasandra did this all of the time. And she did it so fast that no one ever seemed to notice.

As she sat on the couch with her sister's phone in her hand, Kasandra began reading the messages from all of Maria's friends. She read messages about Julie trying out for the cheer squad and Brett going out with Janelle. Then, something caught Kasandra's eye. It was a message from Matthew. Matthew was the 18-year old boy who lived next door with Kasandra's arch enemy, Jessica. Yep, the dreaded Jessica Morrison also happened to be Matthew's younger sister.

Kasandra just had to read the message. Her eyes lit up with shock at the unread message that flashed onto the screen.

Hey Maria. I was wondering if you wanted to go to the pizza place on 5th street sometime. Let me know. Feel free to just give me a call.

"Wow," Kasandra said aloud. "He's asking her on a date!" Kasandra jumped up and started doing a dance.

Hearing all the commotion, Maria stormed into the room and grabbed the phone from Kasandra. "You *had* an unread message…" began Kasandra, obviously guilty of reading her sister's private message. "Sorry," Kasandra said as she slumped down on the couch sadly.

"Wow," said Maria in a breathy voice.

"I know! That was my expression too!" replied Kasandra, now realizing that she probably shouldn't have said anything at all.

"What do I say to him?" Maria asked, as she too sunk into the cushions of the couch.

"Say 'yes!'" replied Kasandra excitedly.

"Okay." Maria shook her head and typed into her phone.

I'm free Friday night…

After a minute of debating with Kasandra about her response, Maria finally pressed the blue send button. Maria sighed and went back to the kitchen for an ice cold glass of water. Kasandra stayed right where she was on the warm, soft, luxurious couch. She soon drifted off to sleep, waking only when she heard her mom walk through the door to start cooking dinner.

Chapter Four

Decision Day

Outside there was a slight chill in the air. It was cold, but at the same time, Kasandra felt warm and light. Fall had just begun, the auburn leaves falling to the ground. It was the weekend, and Kasandra was in the backyard helping her father rake up leaves. Kasandra loved fall. The way the sky looked bluer and the air felt crisper usually relaxed Kasandra. But today, she felt energy coursing through her veins.

After countless jumps off of the neighbors' hill into a pile of leaves, Kasandra saw a figure walking up to her house. Darling was quickly walking over to Kasandra and was holding what seemed to be a letter of some sort. As Darling approached Kasandra, the two girls hugged and walked inside to escape the cool air blowing with the wind.

"So, what did you come over to tell me?" asked Kasandra curiously. Kasandra handed Darling a glass of water just as Darling began to speak.

"So, I need to talk to you about a possible 'life changing event,'" she said.

Almost immediately Kasandra replied, "What kind of 'life changing event' are you talking about?"

"That's the thing," said Darling. "I'm thinking about getting a guide dog."

"Wait, what?" asked Kasandra, who was now even more giddy with curiosity than when she was waiting for her friend to arrive.

"I am talking about a service dog that can help me get around more independently with my blindness."

"Wow," said Kasandra, realizing that this was probably the millionth time she said "wow" today.

"Right now the cane I use is like an extension of my body. It helps me scan for curbs and steps in places that are flat and familiar to me. A guide dog could help me become even more independent. If I get a dog, I'll have to be out of school for a few weeks to do the training. Eleven years old is the youngest age that the school will accept students, and I turn eleven next week. I'll finally be old enough to get a service dog!" Darling took a sip of water from her glass.

"That is so cool, Darling!" exclaimed Kasandra, nearly spilling her drink. Kasandra understood how much being independent meant to her friend.

Darling had told Kasandra before about how she lost her ability to see only a few years ago, but Kasandra didn't stop her friend when she began telling the story once again.

Darling recalled the details of the accident like it had happened yesterday. "My family was very exciting at one time," she began. "When I was little, my parents were scientists. They used to work on cool mysteries, like how to use a spider to make a human life last longer. Now they are just biology professors at Midway College. From a young age, I loved being in the lab with them. It was loads of fun, but my parents thought it was very dangerous. They had trouble keeping me away from the lab, so they decided to secretly move their work to the basement of our house. But soon enough I found out. Of course, I walked in when my parents were performing a radioactive experiment. I wanted to try my own experiment, so I poured something into a vial when no one was looking. Before I could back away, the mixture exploded right in front of my face! All of the juices splashed into my eyes. They quickly became red and dry. My vision went blurry immediately and I was never able to fully recover. My parents quit their jobs as scientists after that, but the damage to my eyes was already done," Darling finished with a small tear in her eye. "Now my parents teach others what they have learned from their years in the lab."

After a quiet moment, Darling asked, "So, do you think I should do it? I mean, my parents said this is a great opportunity and all." The sound of Darling's voice snapped Kasandra back to the present. "I just don't know what to do."

"Well, you came to the right person!" started Kasandra. She grabbed a pencil and notebook from the counter and began flipping through the pages.

"What are you doing?" asked Darling, who appeared to be deep in thought.

"*We* are going to make a list of pros and cons," said Kasandra as she scribbled the words "Pros" and "Cons" on a blank page. She drew a line down the center of the page to separate it into two columns. "So what is one thing that would be good about getting a guide dog?" asked Kasandra, now holding the notebook in front of her as if she was a reporter.

"Well, I would be able to get around better on my own," replied Darling.

"Okay." Kasandra recorded this under the "Pros" column. "So what is something bad about getting a dog?" continued Kasandra, as she prepared to take note of Darling's opinion.

"Well, that's obvious, isn't it? Cleaning up the poop!" Darling giggled. Kasandra wrote it down.

Soon, the two had a pretty hefty list. After a half hour of rock solid thinking, Kasandra set the notebook down in front of them. Kasandra gazed down and read the final list aloud to Darling.

PROS	CONS
• I'll be able to do more on my own	• Cleaning up when it poops
• I won't have to carry a cane	• Only kid at school with a dog
• I'll have a new best friend forever	• My family already has a cat
• The dog will be able to come to school with me	• Being away from my friends for the training
• I will be able to go to new places	• Jessica (she's a con no matter what!)
• I'll feel safer with a friend always by my side	

"Wow!" said Darling, who could easily "see" the answer she already knew in her heart.

"So, what do you think?" Kasandra asked, adding a final, "Yay or nay?"

Darling clasped her hands together and rested them under her chin. "I'll do it," she murmured. Then with much more confidence, Darling exclaimed, "I'm going to do it! I'm going to get a guide dog!"

It was amazing to Kasandra just how quickly Darling's expression had changed as she made her final decision.

"Hooray!" shouted Kasandra, as she did a victory dance once again, similar to the one she did when Matthew asked Maria on a date.

"Yippee!" squealed Darling, joining in on Kasandra's dance.

As the girls were jumping with joy, Maria walked into the kitchen and glanced at them with a confused look on her face. "Ooookay." She continued walking and went out to the back yard. Kasandra and Darling giggled once more.

Anxious to go home and tell her parents about her decision, Darling told Kasandra that it was time for her to leave. "Goodbye and good luck!" said Kasandra, as the two friends hugged one another tightly.

After Darling walked away, Kasandra skipped into her bedroom and thought about spending some time painting or drawing. Instead, Kasandra decided to write in her journal. (For those of you who don't know, there is a fine line between a diary and a journal. A journal is for writing about personal thoughts and feelings. But a diary, this type of journal is used to write about crushes and other drama.) Kasandra picked up a pink pen and began to record her thoughts.

Dear Journal,

Today I found out the most amazing news. Darling is going to a training. What type of training? She will be learning how to use and take care of a seeing eye dog! I'm so happy for her, but I'm also feeling nervous. I am nervous because I don't want a different Darling to come back from the training. She'll have to be away for almost a whole month. Well, it's time for lunch, and I must go!

Enjoy reading my writing!

~ Kasandra Cortez

Chapter Five

Making the Cut

Kasandra woke up the next morning feeling rather happy. She jumped out of bed bright and early. It was Monday, the day that Kasandra would find out if she made the soccer team. Kasandra quickly put on a ruffled blue dress and black flats that had a bow in the center. She pulled her hair up into a sloppy bun before dashing downstairs for breakfast. Kasandra slowed herself and walked into the kitchen. She smiled at her father as she sat down on one of the stools at the island.

"What's up this morning, *querida*?" asked her father, as he cracked an egg into a bowl and started whipping it. *Mmmmmm,* thought Kasandra, as she watched her father prepare toast and cheesy eggs with bacon bits.

Her dad was working a half-day at AT&T, so his outfit seemed to be somewhat casual. He had on a red t-shirt with a dark blue tie, and a pair of jeans. Like Maria and Kasandra, Dad had dark hair. Mom was the only blonde in the family.

As he buttered toast and flipped eggs, Kasandra told her father all about the soccer try outs. Dad's face lit up brightly as he listened to Kasandra speak. He too had played soccer in Brazil when he was Kasandra's age. *I'm glad she's trying activities outside of school instead of keeping to herself. Well, other than Gymnastics,* thought Dad as he placed a plate of food in front of Kasandra.

"*Obrigado,*" she said before biting into a piece of toast.

"You're very welcome," replied Dad. He took off his apron and walked out of the kitchen, stopping first to place a kiss on his youngest daughter's forehead. He could feel himself beaming with pride. Kasandra gobbled up her breakfast, and followed her mother and sister out to Mom's shiny car.

Soon enough, she was following her fellow students through the big blue doors of MaryEllen Bay Middle School. She walked up to her locker just in time to see Darling, John, and Shakira standing there waiting for her.

"You ready?" asked John and Shakira at the same time. Shakira giggled nervously and John just stared at her.

"Yeah, I guess," replied Kasandra, as she stuffed her backpack into the crammed locker.

"I should probably come along too," stated Darling. "Cheer squad and captain positions might also be posted. I bet Jessica's gonna be captain. Again."

"What do you mean by 'again?'" asked Kasandra.

John butted in, "Jessica is captain of the cheer squad every year. It's pretty much expected that she will be again this year."

"But Darling's gonna kick butt this year!" Shakira exclaimed with glee.

"Yeah," said Darling, nervously biting her bottom lip.

The foursome walked by Mrs. Giamoni's classroom where the giant bulletin board was hanging. From a distance, Kasandra could see a paper entitled "MBMS Soccer Team 2017." Shakira and John rushed over to the board and began looking at names and gossiping about them to one another. When Kasandra and Darling finally arrived at the board, Kasandra looked up and pointed to the list. Right there, at the top of the page, printed in the finest print, was her name. "OMG!" she squealed. "I made the team!"

"John and I did too!" exclaimed Shakira, who was practically jumping up and down with joy. Using her hand as a microphone, Shakira said, "Here is the moment of truth, fans. Will Darling make the cut? Or will she crack under pressure?"

"You're not helping." Darling had a worried look on her face. "Is it written in Braille?" she asked seriously.

"No. Would you like me to read it to you?" asked Kasandra.

"Yes, please," replied Darling.

Kasandra began reading the names. "Brianna Danvers, Katrina Wagner, Alexis Mario, and cheer captain is... Darling Adams!"

Kasandra squeaked with happiness as she read her friend's name aloud.

"You've got to be kidding me?" Darling sounded both surprised and overjoyed by the news.

"Well, *she's* not!" said Shakira happily. Just in time to ruin the moment, Jessica waltzed up to the board with Amelia and Katie following her. The click-clack of the girls' high heels was incredibly annoying to Kasandra. She saw Shakira put her hands on her hips and roll her eyes. Shakira turned to Jessica and asked, "What do you want?"

"Oh, I just came to see my name under *Cheer Captain* again," answered Jessica, her attitude harsh and full of spite.

Wow. They really weren't kidding, thought Kasandra.

Shakira smirked as Jessica began to read the list. "Brianna Danvers, Katrina Wagner, Alexis Mario… *WHAT?*" blurted Jessica. Kasandra couldn't help but let out a laugh. Jessica seemed so astonished that she wasn't cheer captain. Jessica grumbled something Kasandra could not hear. "Let's go!" snapped Jessica, marching down the hallway and around the corner with Amelia and Katie right behind her.

"Phew. That was close," said Kasandra.

"You bet," agreed Shakira, as the group walked to Mrs. Miller's math class.

Chapter Six

Disappearing Act

"I have so much homework to do! Who came up with this stuff? When I find out, I'm gonna give them a piece of my mind!" shouted Kasandra angrily.

"Well, you have to practice your math facts, honey," said Mom from the front seat of the car. "It's beautiful outside today, so you and your sister should do your homework in the backyard." Mom always made good suggestions. "How does that sound to you?"

"Yeah. It's fine with me. Ya know, it is almost Halloween. Maybe Maria and I should brainstorm some costume ideas for trick-or-treat."

Lying comfortably beside her older sister on the soft lawn at the back of their house, Kasandra practiced her division facts out loud. "Nine divided by three is three. Four divided by two is two. Sixty-three divided by seven is nine. Ugh. I think that's enough practicing for one day." Kasandra set down her Rocket Math page and turned her attention to Maria. "Do you have any ideas for our Halloween costumes?"

"I was thinking a zombie cheerleader for me," said Maria, quickly pulling up an image on her phone to show Kasandra. When Maria pushed her dainty finger down on the red triangle in the center of the screen, Kasandra realized that her sister was actually showing her a video on YouTube.

A young woman with bright pink hair and dark blue lipstick appeared on the screen. In an animated voice, she began, "Hey, guys! It's Lady Lip, and today I'm going to show you how to do the makeup for a zombie cheerleader disguise!" Kasandra glanced at Maria with a confused look on her face. Lady Lip continued, "First, we are going to do a grey blush on the cheeks. If you want to up your game, you can add some dark blue to create a bruised look. Next, we're going to do a 'smokey eye.' So, we must use black eyeshadow. Take your brush and gently go around the outside of your eye. Add some mascara to complete the final look. And voilà, y'all! You can add scars, cuts, and more bruises to your liking. If you like this video, be sure to check out my YouTube channel. Make sure to press the red subscri-" Maria pressed the home button to close out of the video.

"That's the best tutorial you could find?" questioned Kasandra.

Maria giggled. "Was it really that bad?"

"Um, yeah. It was." Kasandra smiled at her sister before shifting her focus back to the division facts listed on her Rocket Math page. With a sigh, Kasandra flipped over the page and brought up a new conversation.

"Excited for your upcoming date?" Kasandra asked her sister, as she blew her a kiss and drew a heart in the air. Maria's cheeks turned bright red. "Oh! You like him!"

With her finger by her lips, Maria said to her little sister in a loud whisper, "Shush, Kitty!"

"No way!" snickered Kasandra.

The girls gathered up their school work and walked back to the house side-by-side, Kasandra with a knowing grin lighting up her face. Maria dashed upstairs to her bedroom while Kasandra sat down at the kitchen island and grabbed a pack of emoji fruit snacks. Her mother was at the counter carefully chopping up some orange bell peppers. Dad was sitting on the stool next to Kasandra, reading the daily newspaper. "What's up, sweetie?" he asked.

"Nothing much," replied Kasandra, as she opened her snack pack. "Ya know, the poop emojis are my favorite flavored fruit snacks. But, they are my least favorite to eat in public. Don't you agree, Dad?" asked Kasandra, popping an emoji into her mouth.

"Yes, honey," chuckled Dad.

"Don't you agree, Mom?" asked Kasandra.

"Yes, Kasandra," said Mom with a smile, flashing her shiny teeth at her youngest daughter. The three burst into a rain shower of laughter.

Suddenly, Kasandra saw a strange purple light coming from her own hand. *My ring!* She glanced at her parents to see if they had noticed as well. Neither of them were looking in her direction, so Kasandra thought that maybe she could get away to hide in the bathroom before her parents saw her "disappearing act," as Darling and Shakira called it. But Kasandra knew she wouldn't have enough time. Before she disappeared into thin air, all Kasandra managed to say was, "Oops!"

Chapter Seven

Fish Frenzy

Kasandra blinked her eyes and looked around at her surroundings. She found herself lying on a hard, wooden floor. But what exactly did the floor belong to? She stood up and realized that she was on a ship somewhere in the middle of the sea. *Yes! Another mission!* she thought. *But where are the others?*

Kasandra walked around large crates that held different fish. She saw tuna in some and Pacific saury in others. As she quietly moved behind one of the oversized crates, Kasandra spotted John and Shakira lying on the ground below her, their rings shining brightly.

"John? Shakira? Wake up!" she yelled, as she shook her friends by the shoulders one at a time.

"Ah!" screamed Shakira. "What happened?"

"We are on a mission!" Kasandra exclaimed with glee.

"Where's Darling?" asked John, as he began to stand up and look around the ship deck.

"I haven't found her yet. Just you guys."

"We should probably start looking for her," stated Shakira.

"Okay," replied Kasandra, and the three began to search.

The boat appeared to be only about 60 feet long, so Kasandra knew that Darling had to be nearby. After a few moments, Kasandra heard John shout, "I found her!"

Kasandra and Shakira raced over to the spot where the noise was coming from. There was Darling lying in the eastern corner of the boat with a rather confused look on her face. "Is this our second mission?" she asked.

"Probably," responded Shakira. "We seem to be on a fishing boat. But where exactly, I don't know."

John pulled out his phone and began swiping through screens. When he noticed the girls staring at him with questioning expressions, John explained, "I just installed an app that allows anyone to track fishing boats in real time. My dad has been helping a friend watch out for illegal fishing, so he downloaded this cool app. I thought it would be fun to check it out every once in a while too, so I put it on my phone. Maybe it can help us now."

The girls exchanged weary glances as John opened the app and held his phone still. "According to this, we seem to be several miles off the coast of Northern Japan."

"Wow. That's impressive," said Shakira.

Darling nodded, then said very matter-of-factly, "We should go find out what the problem is. Especially before some fishermen show up wondering just who we are."

The foursome bobbed their heads in agreement and stormed out to finish exploring the boat. Kasandra walked through rows of freshly caught fish, the smell making her want to hurl. As the group turned a corner nearby several metal crates, Kasandra noticed a net hanging by a thick cord just below the surface of the water.

"Guys, what's that?" questioned Kasandra, as she and the others approached the unknown item.

"It looks like the net that was probably used to catch all of those fish," said John, as he leaned in closer to examine it in more depth. Everyone stared at him. "What? I went fishing with my dad when I was younger," John explained and shook his head with surprise at the reactions of his friends.

Kasandra took a step closer to John and gazed out at the vast ocean. She settled her eyes on the net that extended from the boat to the water below them. She suddenly grabbed onto John's shoulder in fear as she nearly jumped backwards.

"What is it?" asked Shakira, as she stepped forward to join John and Kasandra at the edge of the deck. Below them in the net were hundreds of silvery fish with bright blue blotches on the undersides of their bodies, but there was also one ginormous fish that seemed to be oddly out of place. "What is *that*?" murmured Shakira.

She moved back to where Darling stood and gave Darling a brief explanation of what they had uncovered.

Darling was quick to respond, "From what you're telling me, it seems like a Pacific white-sided dolphin has gotten caught up in that fishing net."

"A dolphin?" exclaimed John, just beginning to realize that he was part of a now serious conversation.

"Yes, John," Shakira hissed, "a dolphin."

"A Pacific white-sided dolphin avoids tropical or arctic waters. This is neither," reasoned Darling wisely. "Shakira also told me that it is very large. This breed of dolphin can reach a length of seven to eight feet. She told me what it looks like too. A Pacific white-sided dolphin has a white belly, a black beak, and a black ring around each eye. It has to be a Pacific white-sided dolphin! It has to be!" Darling beamed with pride at her identification of the mysterious creature.

"Well, now that we know about the dolphin that needs to be saved, *how* exactly do we save it?" asked John. He was clueless.

"We can't bring the net up because dolphins need water. They are mammals, but they still need the support of the water to help carry their body weight. Keeping the dolphin up in the air until we get it free of the net could make the weight of its body crush its own organs," explained Darling, who was now considering every possible idea. Holding onto every word that Darling spoke, Kasandra stepped forward to hear more. She stopped suddenly and winced in pain.

"Kasandra, are you alr-" started Shakira, rushing to Kasandra's side.

"That's it!" exclaimed Kasandra. She attempted to jump up and down for joy, but found that she could not. She began limping instead.

"What's your idea?" asked Shakira, glancing at the nail jutting out of the wooden deck. It was the same sharp object that had just caused her friend a short burst of pain after stepping on it.

"What if we use a sharp object, like that nail, to saw the net underneath the water? Then the dolphin would be okay without us causing its organs to be crushed," said Kasandra.

"That sounds like a great idea!" replied John.

Kasandra blushed, then said, "On hot summer days back in Brazil, my family and I used to go to the public pool or to the beach. My dad taught me how to swim underwater with my eyes open. I'll do it. I'll go under the water and set the dolphin free. Pool water, salt water, ocean water, or just plain old water... I can do it!"

"That's settled then," said Shakira, as she began to pry the nail from the wood. "There!" she said victoriously, pulling the nail out and handing it to Kasandra.

Examining the item in her hand, Kasandra could see that the point of the nail was razor sharp, like the fang of a Saber-Tooth Tiger. She peeled off her coat and whispered, "I'm ready."

"Here you go," whispered Darling, as she backed up to avoid being splashed. John crossed his fingers, hoping Kasandra would be okay below the surface.

Kasandra took a deep breath in, then jumped overboard, creating a splash and a large ripple in the water. She immediately opened her eyes and found herself surrounded by dark water. She swam smoothly over to the net, yet she could feel the rush of waves rippling over her head. Kasandra heard a faint squeak coming from the trapped dolphin.

"Hurry, Kasandra," breathed Darling from the boat.

Under the water, Kasandra took the nail and began to chisel back and forth on the thin rope of the net. Soon enough, the rope began to break down and small fish rapidly started to escape from the net. Kasandra continued to work to break down the rope until she had created a hole large enough to allow the dolphin to swim out. Kasandra motioned to the rubbery mammal to swim free, and it did. She watched the beautiful creature swish away from her.

All at once, hundreds of tiny fish swarmed out of the net and into Kasandra's direction. The rush of fast fish knocked the wind out of her. Everything went black as Kasandra floated motionlessly beneath the surface of the chilly Pacific Ocean.

What happened next, no one really knows, except for Kasandra of course. Although even Kasandra couldn't say what was going through the dolphin's mind in that very moment.

Suddenly, a rush of water pressured Kasandra from behind, pushing her to the surface of the deep water. Almost immediately, Kasandra gasped for air. She felt the wind rushing around her. She looked down and saw the slick body of the gorgeous Pacific white-sided dolphin beneath her. Kasandra threw her hands in the air and let out a loud "woo-hoo!"

The dolphin swam up to Kasandra's side and she carefully wrapped her arms around its shiny body. Kasandra rode the dolphin safely back to the boat where she climbed up a rope ladder that John and Shakira had found and lowered while she was gone. Darling embraced Kasandra with a warm hug the moment she was back aboard the dry ship.

"We did it!" exclaimed Kasandra.

"How did you stay under water that long, Kasandra?" asked John in complete awe of the talented girl standing in front of him.

"I came up to the surface a few times to catch my breath, ya know," replied Kasandra with a wink. The group giggled and high-fived one another.

Kasandra knew it was time for the foursome to end their journey. "Now, let's get out of here before we run into any illegal fisherman," she said.

Before walking away from the now empty fishnet, Kasandra picked up a Pacific saury and dropped it over the railing. It landed right in the patient dolphin's open mouth. Kasandra smiled down at her new friend and said, "Now, you stay out of trouble. I might never see you again, but know that the Animal Guard will always be there for you. So goodbye, my friend." She waved farewell, then walked over to where her friends were gathered.

Kasandra placed her hand with the glowing ring in the center of the circle. The others followed her lead. In a poof, they disappeared, only to find themselves standing in their own headquarters, looking into a large computer monitor. On the screen was the face of the one and only Miss Caroline Kalisto staring back at them.

Chapter Eight

Gadgets and Distractions

The woman sat at her usual desk, the "Secretary of Recruits" sign shining on the corner of the desk. "Hello agents," she said in her low voice. From what Kasandra understood, Miss Kalisto was very serious. She had dark skin and poofy hair that stuck out on both ends of her head.

"Hi!" replied Kasandra enthusiastically, expecting an on-point pep talk.

"Congratulations on the mission."

Just as soon as Miss Kalisto began talking, Shakira jumped in front of the computer screen. "Just another trophy to add to our shelves," she exclaimed. The group laughed. Well, everyone but Miss Kalisto laughed.

"Very funny, Agent Umbridge," said Miss Kalisto, her tone oozing with sarcasm. "As I was saying," she continued, "These missions... they've been, well... a distraction."

Kasandra's jaw dropped lower than it ever had before, while all John could say was, "What? All that work... for nothing?"

At first no words came out of Darling's mouth. Nothing. Finally, in a quiet mumble, Darling spoke. "What do you mean by 'a distraction?'"

"These missions you have been going on... well, they are simply the kindergarten of missions. They've been distractions from learning more about Crow and Vulture," Miss Kalisto reasoned. "The small missions have been disguising the fact that these criminals are out there, whether we here at the Animal Guard like it or not. We've been watching your team. We feel you are ready to enter stage two of this project." Miss Kalisto smirked. "But first, you'll need some gadgets."

"What gadgets?" Kasandra wondered aloud.

"Those," replied Miss Kalisto, as she pointed to a row of tools laid out behind Kasandra and her friends. The objects had appeared right behind them and no one had even noticed! The group moved closer to the mysterious items. "First, on your left, is amnesia spray. One spritz and that person will forget the past hour. It's simple. One spritz equals one hour gone."

Kasandra gently picked up the bottle with the large green sticker labeling it "Amnesia Spray." It looked like water, only it had a sweet rose perfume smell to it. Kasandra passed it to Shakira, who passed it to John, who passed it to Darling.

"Next, is an agent tracker that my unit uses," Miss Kalisto informed them, as she once again pointed to an object on the floor. It was tiny and also had a green sticker on it. The sticker read, "Agent Tracker." Miss Kalisto continued, "Now, you must listen carefully. Pick up the tracker and look on the back of it. Peel off the paper that you see to reveal a sticky back. Now, place it under your ring."

Kasandra did as Miss Kalisto instructed. "This will allow me to know where you are at all times. This won't tell *you* where you are, but it will tell me. Do you understand?" asked Miss Kalisto sternly.

"Yes," replied the group, as each one of them securely placed the tiny device on the backsides of their rings.

"Very good. Now, onto the next gadget," Miss Kalisto continued. "This object is a smoke bomb. It is an easy distraction to help you escape at bad times during a mission. The bomb will explode if it is dropped, stepped on, or thrown." Unlike the other objects, this gadget looked like a ball. This was one of Kasandra's favorite gadgets shown to the team. It reminded her of the hit TV show *K.C. Undercover*.

"Lastly," said Miss Kalisto, who was now looking at a small pen laying on the floor. Kasandra and her friends followed her gaze to the pen, but what really caught their eye was the way the pen looked. It appeared to be an average, shiny, black pen with the usual jet black ink. Miss Kalisto continued, "This is a Motion Minimizing Device, or M.M.D. for short. Do you want to know how to use it?"

"Oh, yes!" replied Kasandra.

Miss Kalisto smiled. Well, if you believe it was a smile. "Agent Martin?"

"Yes?" asked John.

"Grab that ball." She pointed to a bouncy-ball that Kasandra had left on the floor after playing with it earlier in the week.

"Okay." John walked over to it, picked it up, then returned to the computer screen.

"Agent Umbridge, you grab the pen and do as I say." Shakira picked up the pen in a heartbeat and waited for the next instruction. "Agent Umbridge, I want you to press down on the top of the pen so the tip comes out. Before you do this though, Agent Martin will toss the ball in the air. You will aim at it, and the pen will do its thing."

They nodded and Shakira got the pen ready for action. With Miss Kalisto's nod of approval, John tossed the ball into the air while Shakira pressed down on the pen. A small beam of light came out of the tip of the pen. Then, it stopped the ball in mid-air, letting it fall slowly to the ground. The ball was falling in slow motion. *This is amazing!* Kasandra said to herself moments later when the ball finally reached the ground.

"And those are your new gadgets," Miss Kalisto stated proudly.

"So, now that we know what we'll be working with, could we maybe get back to the distraction thingy?" questioned Kasandra.

Miss Kalisto sighed. "I believe so. While you all were on that boat there was trouble somewhere else. It's classified information, but

I can tell you that the Animal Guard has been trying to catch the villains Crow and Vulture. I can also tell you that your mission was just a simple prank compared to whatever they're planning. Hence, a distraction."

"Wow! Hold on," exclaimed John, stepping closer to the computer monitor. "What you're saying is that Crow and Vulture could be out there, *ARE* out there, planning who knows what, while we're rescuing dolphins and zebras?"

"Exactly, Agent Martin," replied Miss Kalisto promptly. "That is why our meeting is over." With that, Kasandra and her friends vanished.

"Welcome to graduation," breathed Miss Kalisto, her image still flashing on the big screen. She reached out her hand and switched off the computer, leaving the empty room dark.

Chapter Nine

Not Paris

"Ahhhh!" screamed Kasandra, her arms flailing wildly as she plummeted to the ground. She landed with a *thud* from the six foot drop. Without even bothering to wipe the dirt and dry grass off of her body, Kasandra pulled herself up from the ground and rushed over to her friends.

"Where on Earth are we now?" shouted Darling.

"Well, it's not Paris, that's for sure. Why can't we end up in Paris for once?" Shakira whined. With a smile and a wink, she added, "Do you have an app for this, John?"

The group laughed, and John's face turned red like a tomato. However, John's expression turned serious as he looked to their left. The friends' laughter quickly faded. "I don't think we need one to know where we are." John pointed to a mob of kangaroos hopping through the long grass.

"Wow!" gasped Shakira. "Are those...?"

"Yep." Kasandra looked at her friends suspiciously. "The real question isn't what they are or where we are. It's *what* we are doing here that should scare us."

Darling nodded. "What now?"

"Kangaroos," said Kasandra, as she turned to face the mob. "Let's take a look around." The others followed and they quietly moved closer to the animals. They saw about six kangaroos and four joeys. *Ten kangaroos. How bad can that be?* Kasandra thought to herself.

The grass was up to their knees now, but they cautiously ventured on until they were close enough to see the sharp claws and the bulging leg muscles of the Australian animals. They had cone-shaped faces and pearly eyes. Kasandra stopped dead in her tracks, causing Shakira and Darling to crash into her back.

"What's wrong?" Darling and Shakira whispered in unison. Shakira reached down to help John up from the ground. He had tried to dodge the girls' collision, but instead landed on his butt.

"Look." Kasandra's friends all turned to look in the same direction as Kasandra, their eyes widening with surprise. As they peered at the largest kangaroo's eyes, they noticed that its eyes were *red*. Bright, blood red.

Shakira told Darling what they were all seeing before them, and John asked, "Is that normal?"

"Please tell me it's normal!" pleaded Kasandra, shaking her head in disbelief. "This is really happening, isn't it?"

"Oh, that's not normal at all," whispered Darling.

As the group looked around to inspect the eyes of the other kangaroos, they saw that they were all the same. "It's like they're possessed," murmured John.

"Tell me about it!" exclaimed Shakira. Her voice rose with fear. "Now what? We're dealing with evil spirits and hypnotists?" Shakira quickly covered her mouth. But it was too late. The group of crazed kangaroos turned to them, their eyes glowing fiercely.

"Uh-oh," breathed Kasandra. "What are we gonna do, guys?"

"I have an idea!" said Shakira in a low, soft voice. "Darling, do you remember our research project back in the first grade?"

Darling's face lit up. "Yeah… it was on…"

"Kangaroos!" interrupted John. Only seconds later did he realize that he shouldn't have said anything.

"How… why… but… how did you know about our project?" stuttered Shakira. "You weren't even in our class."

"We're neighbors, Shakira, for goodness sake!"

"Oh, what are you now, my personal stalker?" asked Shakira wildly.

"I just heard your mom talking to my parents. That doesn't make me a stalker! I'm just an active eavesdropper! I, uh,…"

Kasandra quickly cut him off, bringing the team back to the moment. "How about Darling and Shakira tell us about their project so maybe, just maybe, we can find a way to startle the angry, uh, possessed mob of kangaroos!"

John glared at Kasandra, although he knew she was right. They needed to get to work.

Shakira began, "So, kangaroos are fast. Their hops are also very powerful because they use their strong legs to move. So really, they could be over here at any second."

Suddenly, Kasandra remembered something that Miss Kalisto told them earlier that day. *"This last object is a smoke bomb. It is an easy distraction to help you escape at bad times during a mission."*

"That's it!" Kasandra exclaimed. "The smoke bomb!"

"But where is it?" asked John with a puzzled, yet determined, look on his face.

The group started looking on the ground and in the plants around them when Kasandra felt something abruptly drop into her pocket. She looked down and took a peek inside. Kasandra began jumping up and down chanting "Yes! Yes! Yes!" She removed the tiny metal ball from her pocket and prepared herself to throw it in the direction of the kangaroos.

"WAIT!" Shakira ran up to Kasandra and grabbed the gadget from her. "What are we going to do after we throw it?" Shakira asked Kasandra, refusing to give the smoke bomb back until they had a fully developed plan of action.

"I don't know," sighed Kasandra sadly. "Where *won't* kangaroos go?"

"Well, they're faster than us," stated John.

"And they're stronger," added Darling.

Kasandra thought for a moment. "Can kangaroos climb trees?"

"I don't know. There is only one way to find out," said Shakira, giving the gadget back to Kasandra with a smile. Kasandra smiled back and then threw the smoke bomb as far as she possibly could. It successfully made it to where the angry kangaroos stood, surrounding them with a dark cloud of smoke. It would take the bewildered kangaroos a few minutes to realize that Kasandra and her friends were gone.

The wind was blowing in Kasandra's face as she sprinted towards the nearest tree. John was ahead of her, and Shakira followed, holding Darling's hand to help guide her. John climbed swiftly up the first few branches, pulling Kasandra up high into the tree with him. She smiled at him, then began to help John pull up Darling and Shakira. Once they were huddled safely in the branches of the tree, they decided that they needed a better plan than just hiding out in a tree.

"What now?" asked Shakira, as she peered through the thick layer of leaves surrounding them.

Kasandra cautiously moved closer to the branch where Shakira sat and joined her in gazing out at the Australian wilderness. She looked down and noticed that the mob of kangaroos was gone. "They're gone, you guys!" Everyone's heads perked up and smiles of relief spread across their faces.

All of a sudden, Kasandra heard a scream. She knew it was John's scream. Unlike most of the boys she knew, John didn't have a low, manly scream. Instead it was a high-pitched, girly scream. Kasandra turned around and began to laugh at what she saw. Darling and Shakira started to laugh too! There was John, curled up in a ball, looking up at the branches above them, staring into the face of an angry koala bear.

"Why me, little guy? What did I do?" he pleaded, trying to avoid the soul-catching eyes of the koala. Kasandra thought the koala's eyes were rather cute. They looked like chocolate chips on a gray, furry cookie.

"Awww! How cute!" squealed Shakira, moving closer to it. The koala had now made its way down to face Shakira. "Hi, little guy! What's your name?"

"Shakira, we're in the wild," pointed out John.

"I'm trying to save you right now, John, from this adorable fluff-ball," Shakira giggled. The koala moved quickly. (After all, koala bears can run up to 20 miles per hour!) The koala weaved its way around Shakira's hips and got into a comfortable position, wiggling like a small child. When it was done moving it looked like a large baby in Shakira's arms.

"*Que fofo!* It loves you, Shakira!" exclaimed Kasandra.

Shakira hugged the koala closely and said, "I'm going to call you Keith. Yeah, Keith the koala."

After a good laugh, the group decided that they should leave Keith's tree and try to save the kangaroos from the trance they were in. Kasandra hopped out of the tree and the foursome waved goodbye to their furry friend. Then, the strangest thing happened. Keith waved back at them.

"Bye, then!" came a voice with a heavy Australian accent from behind the group. Kasandra spun around on her heels. It was Keith. He was talking!

Chapter Ten

Crow and Vulture

The group froze. No one said a word. Well, except for Keith. Kasandra's eyes widened as Keith's mouth opened yet again.

"What you gonna do? Leave me out here all 'lone?"

Kasandra couldn't resist the urge to tell Keith the truth. "Well, yes. But, you see, we kind of have to save the kangaroo species, so…"

"I'm Shakira, and this is Darling, John, and Kasandra. Pleased to make your acquaintance," said Shakira with a curtsy.

"Yeah, yeah. Alright then. My name is Mojo, by the way." He glared at Shakira. "Now back to the thing about saving the kangaroo species. Can I come along?"

Kasandra felt this question coming on from the beginning. She knew what to say. "Keith, uh, Mojo," she corrected herself. "For your own safety, we don't want you to come with us. It's for the safety of your entire species really."

"Well, then," said the animal, seeming surprised.

"I know this might be shocking, Mojo, but you need to stay calm," said Kasandra.

"I'm not shocked. I'm excited!" exclaimed the delighted koala.

"You still can't come," Kasandra told him, hoping he would just give it up soon.

But then Mojo did something that surprised Kasandra and her friends even more than when he started talking to them earlier. Mojo came down from the tree to the ground, sat down, then made a face. Not just any face, but a pouty face. His eyes appeared to get large, even though the eyes of a koala are actually tiny. He stuck out his lower lip until he heard someone say, "Okay. I guess it won't hurt if you tag along." It was John. Everyone was shocked, even Mojo, because the boy who was scared of the creature only moments before now wanted him to stay with them.

"Okay, then. This has been settled. Mojo, you are allowed to come with us," Kasandra said, as she began to look around her again. "What next?" she muttered so softly that no one heard. Then the idea hit her. "I know what to do! We could split up and take a look around, to see if we can find out any possible ways to help the kangaroos."

Darling shrugged. "Sounds good to me," she said with a smile.

"Shakira and Darling! You guys can go east. John, Mojo, and I will go west. We can meet back here in one hour. Okay?" Kasandra looked at her friends hoping that they would agree with her plan.

"Okay," said the group in perfect harmony. Kasandra smiled, knowing that she had the world's most perfect team of friends. And with that, the group moved out, ready to tackle their newest adventure.

Kasandra moved west with John and Mojo, lifting every rock, pebble, or boulder she could, trying to find the cause of the kangaroo possession. Mojo hung onto John's back like a sloth. Kasandra noticed that the koala was strangely sound asleep. "Mojo?" she asked, tapping him on the shoulder.

"What do you want?" he asked with annoyance.

"Why are you sleeping? It's only 4 PM!" she exclaimed.

"Ah, dearie! Don't you know koalas sleep nearly 22 hours each day?"

"So, koalas are only awake for 2 hours every day?"

"Yep. You got that right, La-sandra!" he said, as he began to doze off again.

"It's Kasandra, not La-sandra," Kasandra spouted, getting a little irritated by him.

"I think your name's pretty. Kasandra or La-sandra," said John with a smile.

Kasandra knew the last part of his sentence was supposed to be a joke, so she laughed. "Thanks, John. I appreciate it."

The group kept moving forward, exploring the beautiful Australian life that surrounded them.

Darling and Shakira puffed their way to a clearing about a mile from where they had started at Mojo's tree. As they walked on the dry soil, Darling asked Shakira, "Hey, um, do you know what we are looking for?"

"No clue."

"Oh, ok. Just wondering."

As they continued walking, neither girl noticed their path getting rockier, littered by pebbles the size of a penny. Shakira walked ahead of Darling, and as the rocks became bigger, Shakira tripped over one, landing flat on her face. "Ouch!" she yelled, examining her leg. "Nothing to worry about. Just a scratch," she assured her friend (and herself!).

Shakira was about to get up when she noticed two black dots bobbing up and down in the sky. "Oh no! Darling, we need to get out of here!" she yelled, grabbing Darling's hand and leading the way as they sprinted back towards Mojo's tree.

"Well, it's been almost an hour," said Kasandra, turning around with John and Mojo.

The walk back to Mojo's tree was quiet, considering that Kasandra, John, and Mojo were all usually pretty loud. Especially Mojo.

"Are we there yet?" the impatient koala asked repeatedly.

"Are you off of my back yet?" snapped John. Kasandra couldn't help but let out a small giggle.

When they arrived back at Mojo's tree, Kasandra thought it odd that Darling and Shakira were back at the tree before them. "Huh?" she muttered to herself before asking them how they got back so early.

"You won't believe this! I saw Crow and Vulture!" rambled Shakira in an almost excited way.

"What? Who?" questioned Mojo, jumping off of John's back and into the tree.

John let out a sigh of relief to have the koala off of his back, then said, "I can't believe this!"

"I know! That's why I clearly stated 'You won't believe this!'" replied Shakira.

"How did you find them?" asked Kasandra at the same time that John questioned, "What did they look like?"

"I'm getting to that part, John," said Shakira with a glare. She continued, "So, Darling and I were walking along a stone path. It started to get real rocky and I tripped on one of the rocks and got this scratch." Shakira pointed to the small gash on her right leg. "When I looked up, I saw these two dots moving up and down in the sky. I knew they had to be birds, but I still had to find out what type of birds they were. Then, I remembered looking at pictures of birds with my dad when I was younger. We used to go bird watching together before he went back to the military. I almost automatically knew that one was a crow and the other was a vulture. This can't be a coincidence, can it? I mean, what are the odds that we see a crow flying next to a vulture on the same mission that brought us crazed kangaroos?" Shakira paused to take a deep breath. She felt like she had talked for a long time, even though she considered talking so much to be one of her many talents.

"So, what did they look like exactly?" asked Darling.

"I don't know. Uh, they looked like normal birds, I guess," stuttered Shakira.

"Okay. So they weren't human is what you're saying. Right, Shakira?" Darling asked, seeking some clarification before ending her interrogation.

"Yes. They were definitely birds," finished Shakira, taking another deep breath.

Kasandra began to pull the puzzle pieces of information they had together, and came up with a hypothesis about what was happening to the kangaroos. "So, um, maybe Crow and Vulture only have to do with part of our mission, like when we got the dolphin out of the net earlier. Stuff like that happens all of the time. But then I think Crow and Vulture have something to do with this mission too because kangaroos don't just happen to get red eyes when they eat food. Right?"

The group looked confused at first, but then they all nodded in agreement.

"Crow and Vulture, eh? Sounds like comic book characters to me," Mojo chimed in.

"What? You know who they are?" Kasandra quickly asked, turning in Mojo's direction.

"We koalas have seen 'em before. Years ago though. We know a thing or two 'cause we've seen a thing or two."

"We are Farmers! Bum, ba, dum, bum, bum, bum, bum!" sang John, breaking the serious tone of the group for a second.

Mojo once again made a face that no one ever thought a koala could do. This time he looked confused. Everyone laughed. Then John explained the joke. "It's a song from a commercial for an insurance agency." The friends' faces were almost purple from laughing so hard.

"Okay. So, do we think they have something to do with the kangaroos?" Shakira asked.

"Yeah. I mean, who else has the time to create a kangaroo army?" Kasandra replied, sparking more laughter from the group.

"Nice one, Kasandra! A kangaroo army!" said John between Darling and Shakira's giggles.

"Guys! I'm serious!" Kasandra practically yelled at them. Everyone became silent and turned their gazes towards her. Kasandra put her hands over her mouth. Even she was shocked at what she said when they were just having a little bit of fun. "I'm sorry, guys. I just thought a little less laughing would help us stay safe from Crow and Vulture. Maybe they won't be able to find us here," Kasandra said apologetically.

"It's okay," Darling said, placing her delicate hand on Kasandra's shoulder.

"Thanks."

"You're welcome," Darling replied with a warm smile.

"Now, then," began Kasandra. "We need a plan." She smiled. "So, here's what we know." Kasandra grabbed a stick and began drawing in the dirt. "We have an evil kangaroo army on the loose, and we are pretty sure that Crow and Vulture are somehow involved. Shakira, what direction were they going?"

Shakira thought for a second. "North, I think."

"So, therefore, we need to head, uh, Shakira, which direction did you and Darling go?"

"East!" Shakira exclaimed with a "You came up with the plan" look.

Kasandra gave her an "I'm sorry" look back, then said, "So, we all move east until the path gets rockier. Then, we move north. Got it?"

"Got it!" the group replied in unison.

They began to walk east together. Only moments later, the group paused. "What's that?" asked Shakira, pointing to a small bird up in one of the nearby trees.

"That's a kookaburra. It's one of the native birds of Australia," stated John. Then, he added, "What? I don't just have a boat app. I have a safari one too!"

Shakira smirked. "We are sorry we misjudged you, John." In almost perfect harmony, Shakira, Darling, and Kasandra all stuck out their lower lips forming pouty faces just like Mojo had given them. *Where is Mojo?* thought Kasandra. She turned around to see Mojo sprinting over to them.

"Eh? 'Ello?" he practically screamed. Kasandra giggled, then rushed over to him. Mojo hopped onto Kasandra's back.

"Sorry about that, Mojo. It won't happen again," she assured him with another giggle. Soon enough, Mojo was fast asleep where he rested on her back.

Hearing Mojo's gentle snores, the group decided to stop for a moment to take a break. "Let's keep going," Kasandra told them after only a one-minute rest.

"She's right. We're almost there," said Shakira.

Together, the group continued to venture into the vast Australian outback.

Chapter Eleven

Possessed

It wasn't long before the path became rockier, more dangerous with every step. Kasandra looked down and flipped over a large stone.

Shakira shifted her attention to the ground. "This is it," she informed the adventurers, pointing to the beat up rock. "This is where I fell. That's the rock that tripped me."

They turned towards the north, only to see the same setting. When you think of the scary "Do Not Enter" sign in a fairytale, you think it is a dark, spooky setting, with lightning bolts smashing into the ground. But, this scene wasn't that. Instead, it was bright and sunny, warm, and the sky was blue. Large, cumulus clouds floated in the sky like pieces of cotton candy.

Kasandra gulped. "No matter what, we have to stick together. We are a team." Her fellow teammates looked at one another, then over at Kasandra. They all nodded in agreement. Kasandra could feel the dried up grass crunch under her feet with every step that she took. *You got this*, she told herself as she continued to move forward.

They walked for another mile or so until they came to a cluster of trees sitting there, as if they had been waiting for Darling, John, Shakira, and Kasandra to arrive. Kasandra walked into the center of the cluster, her allies following closely behind. The leaves were not golden like the ones in the United States at this time of year. Instead, they were still a bright green color. *Wow! This is amazing!* Kasandra told herself as she gazed longingly at the beautiful trees.

There were no signs of Crow and Vulture anywhere. "This is so beautiful, yet so strange," Kasandra said, turning to face her friends.

"Yeah," breathed Shakira. She wandered closer to the trees.

Kasandra spun in circles looking for any possible clue or sign that Crow and Vulture had been there.

"Hey, guys! I think I found something!" shouted Shakira triumphantly. Darling, Kasandra, and John moved over towards Shakira, hoping for good news. "Look at this tree."

"Okay," said Kasandra slowly, looking at the tree just like Shakira had told her to. Kasandra continued to look at it (well, more like stare at it!), but all she could find were long lines carved into the bark.

"Do you see it yet?" asked Shakira, anxious for her friends to see what she had found.

"Can you please just tell us?" Darling questioned, trying to remind Shakira that she could not "see" whatever it was no matter how hard she tried.

"Oh, yeah," Shakira began. "See these lines?" The group nodded. "These, over here, create a triangle-like shape, while these create..." She stopped speaking for a second.

Kasandra saw the hidden picture! When she was about to say something, John exclaimed, "Oh! Oh! I got it! It's 'The Illumanati!'"

"Way to go, John," replied Shakira sarcastically.

"Really?" he asked.

"No!" Shakira practically yelled at him. "It's a 'C' and a 'V,' for 'Crow' and 'Vulture!'" shouted Shakira wildly. The group gasped in disbelief.

"I wonder what will happen if I touch it," John said, reaching his hands out to feel the hard, wooden surface.

"John! No!" shouted Shakira.

But it was too late. When his fingers touched the trunk of the tree, the surface moved slightly inward like the pressing of a button.

Just then, a gust of wind blew up, sending sand and other small minerals spiraling around them. All of a sudden, Kasandra let out a loud sneeze. (Of course, when humans sneeze, an involuntary reflex is triggered that causes them to briefly close their eyes as they let out that "a-choo.") As Kasandra released that single sneeze, she closed her eyes for just a split-second.

Kasandra, however, did not know any of this happened as she became caught in a storm of sneezes. "A-choo! A-choo! Aaa-choo!" she sneezed repeatedly. Then, she stopped. The whole circle fell quiet. Or at least that's what Kasandra thought. "Sorry about that, guys. I have bad allergies when it comes to pollen, sand, and some other stuff," she explained. They all just stood there, as if frozen in time. As if waiting for a command. *Command! No!* The words echoed in Kasandra's mind.

"Kasandra? What's wrong with them?" asked a small, quiet voice from just to the left of Kasandra.

"Darling! Thank goodness!" Kasandra jumped up and hugged Darling as hard as she possibly could.

"So," said Darling, smiling after the hug from her dear friend. "What happened?"

"Well, John and Shakira seem to be possessed. I'm not quite sure how, but I think that Crow and Vulture are controlling them somehow, just like with the kangaroos," Kasandra stated.

"Oh," Darling replied. "Why am I not possessed then? And what about you?"

"I think it might have something to do with our eyes," Kasandra thought out loud.

"Oh! That makes perfect sense! I can't see, so I wasn't affected. But, uh, how are you not under the control of Crow and Vulture?" Darling asked cautiously.

Kasandra shrugged. "I don't really know." Then, she remembered something. About a year ago, Kasandra and Maria were drinking Snapple iced tea in their old house back in Brazil. When Kasandra opened her bottle, "Real Fact #395" was written under the cap. It read, "It is impossible to sneeze with your eyes open." Now Kasandra understood. "I've got it!"

"What did you figure out?" asked Darling eagerly.

Kasandra thrilled Darling with her adventures in drinking Snapple, then got to the point. "So, I'm not being controlled because my eyes were closed when I had that sneezing fit. That must have been when this 'possession' happened to John and Shakira." It all made sense to Kasandra now. The answer was clear. But now it meant that it was up to her and Darling alone to save their friends… and the entire kangaroo species.

"Ka-, uh, should we use our code names now?" asked Darling. "Crow and Vulture could be close."

"Sure, Daring Deer. Do you know where Mojo is?" Kasandra walked around for a few seconds before finding Mojo. He appeared to be frozen too, just waiting to be told what to do, but oddly, he was in a handstand position. Kasandra let out a short giggle, then walked back over to Darling. "He's over there," Kasandra pointed, then said, "a few feet to your right."

"Got it, Kitty."

Kasandra smiled. She liked having Darling around. Just then the thought occurred to her that soon Darling would be gone, learning how to use a guide dog. Remembering this gave Kasandra the idea to throw Darling a surprise party before she left for her training. *Yeah, that's what I'll do! I'll plan it with John and Shakira once we get out of this mess. I guess Mojo could come too, but I can't afford a plane ticket, so neither can he.*

Kasandra frowned for a second. She looked back at where her friends stood, remembering the terrible situation that was currently happening right there in Australia.

"Hey, Daring Deer?"

Darling's head perked up right at the moment she heard Kasandra say her code name. "Yeah?"

"Do you think it's possible that there could be something inside of this tree?"

Darling's face lit up. "That's a great idea! Let's see if we can somehow open it up, Kitty."

Kasandra giggled. "Alright!"

"How do we open the tree, ur," Darling frowned. "You know what I mean. So, um, how do we get a look inside without setting off the possessing light show?"

"I'm not quite sure," said Kasandra, drifting off into the endless stream of her thoughts. "What if it needs some sort of recognition? I mean, how else do people keep stuff protected these days? There's a phone that requires face ID for goodness sake!" This all came out of Kasandra's mouth so quickly that she didn't get to

71

think too much about it. However, once it was out, she knew it was brilliant. Darling thought so too.

"That's actually a pretty good idea, Kitty! To do, like, the recognition thing, don't we need something that belongs to Crow and Vulture?"

"I think so," replied Kasandra. She looked up into the blue sky, then asked, "In order for all of this to happen, Crow and Vulture must have been here at some point, right?"

"I guess so," reasoned Darling.

"Then, Daring Deer, I suppose we should start looking for a clue, or for something that they left behind." Kasandra walked around the tree looking for this big clue, even if that meant it was really something tiny. Everything mattered now, regardless of size.

Darling and Kasandra looped around the trees, looking and feeling for anything that could help them solve this puzzle. But they ended up right back where they started.

"Let's go farther down the path," suggested Kasandra. Darling nodded and the girls moved past the trees, entering a land completely foreign to them. They continued their journey for another quarter of a mile until a shiny spot on the ground caught Kasandra's eye. On the ground, right below her foot, was a glossy black feather. Almost automatically, Kasandra bent down and picked it up. Without warning, she grabbed Darling's hand and together they bolted back to where the mystifying tree stood.

Chapter Twelve

The Evil Chip

Wind rushed past Kasandra once again as she and Darling made their way all the way back to where John and Shakira stood motionlessly by the strange tree.

"Daring Deer, we did it! We got a feather!" she exclaimed, hugging her friend with joy.

"What if it doesn't work?" asked Darling nervously.

"I guess we'll see!" said Kasandra, sounding almost as nervous as Darling.

Kasandra held Darling's hand as the two girls lightly pressed the feather up against the mysterious tree trunk. Kasandra closed her eyes and took a deep breath. Nothing happened. "What?" she muttered. She spoke too soon. Instead of a light flashing in their eyes, the tree began to act like a robot. It slowly creaked open, revealing its metal insides to the girls.

"Wow," Kasandra heard Darling say softly at the sound of creaking metal. Kasandra laughed nervously.

The metal was inches thick, the layers piling up. Once all of the layers finished opening up, a tiny silver chip was all that remained inside the hollowed-out tree. "That must be it then. This little chip must be what is controlling the kangaroos... and our friends," Kasandra said, taking a step forward and reaching out to grab it.

"Kitty!"

"What, Daring Deer?" asked Kasandra, slowly pulling her hand away from the tree, if you could even call it a tree anymore.

"You're too impulsive, just like The Parrot," Darling scolded.

"What do you mean?" asked Kasandra. Although, she quickly realized that there was truly no need for the current argument.

Darling let out a small smile. "You and The Parrot... you both try to get right down to the point too fast. You don't try to figure things out completely. Take it slow."

Kasandra took a deep breath, then nodded an "OK" to Darling. As much as Kasandra didn't want to admit it, Darling was right. This was a way that she and John were similar. They were both fast-paced, and as Darling had said, they "both try to get right down to the point," maybe too fast sometimes. Kasandra thought for a moment. Maybe this is what made her like John a lot more than most people did (other than his own family, of course!).

"Okay," began Darling. "Let's think. Um. So, the last time we touched anything without thinking first, it was rigged. We lost Round

1. So, in Round 2 of 'the Animal Guard vs. the Mechanical Tree,' we need to be more careful and act with caution. This chip could be rigged too."

Kasandra nodded once more and began to think. *Okay. We can do this. We need a plan. Then we can get our friends back and go home and rest... and plan a surprise party!* That's when the idea came to her. *Rest... the art of taking it SLOW!*

"Darling? I have a plan!" she exclaimed. "Oops. Sorry. I forgot about code names for a second," Kasandra said apologetically.

Darling gave her an "it's OK" look, then began to listen to Kasandra as she told her all about her brilliant plan.

Right as Kasandra opened her mouth to speak again, she was stunned by the sight of the kangaroo army rapidly approaching them.

Darling was startled by the sound of their feet hitting the ground. "Great!" she yelled, throwing her hands up in the air.

"I guess we need to move quicker than I thought," Kasandra said to Darling, as she turned to once again face the mechanical tree. Just as she did this, the kangaroos stopped in their tracks. Then, John, Shakira, and Mojo began to hop. Yep, that's right, H-O-P, hop. They hopped in the direction of the kangaroos until they reached them. Then, something really strange happened. John bent down and began to munch on the grass, as if it was a late afternoon snack. Kasandra couldn't help but let out a giggle. She could tell that Darling had some trouble resisting the laughter stuck inside of her too when Kasandra told her why she was giggling.

"Okay. Back to the plan," Kasandra insisted, snapping back into save-the-world mode.

Turning her attention back to the situation before them, Kasandra said to Darling with a lingering smile, "Slowly... Daring Deer! That's it! You did it!"

Darling looked confused. "What did I do?"

"You told me I move too quickly... so what if we slow the kangaroos down using the M.M.D.? Then we will have more time to get the chip out of the tree!"

"Oh, yeah. I did think of that!" Darling replied victoriously. The girls giggled, and Kasandra once again reached into her pocket and pulled out another object. It was the M.M.D., or the Motion Minimizing Device. Kasandra yanked the pen out of her pocket, and then had to remember what Miss Kalisto told her to do to use the slow motion piece of technology. Kasandra did as her instructor had told her to, by clicking the top of the pen, causing the small tip to come out of the pen. Then, almost immediately, a blast shot out of the pen's tip, aiming straight for the angry kangaroos. Suddenly, the mob actually slowed down as they hopped, now taking them nearly one minute to complete each hop.

Kasandra gasped with worry. "Uh, Daring Deer?" Darling turned towards Kasandra. "The Parrot and Peacock Princess... they're hopping slowly too," she said, remembering to use her friends' code names as well. She couldn't take it. She had to laugh. Never in her wildest dreams had Kasandra thought she would say that last sentence. Or any sentence that she had said on this entire mission!

After Kasandra finished laughing, she looked at Darling and told her, "Let's go climb up that tree over there, so the kangaroos won't see us for a while. When they think that we are gone, we come back out, and get that chip. We've delayed the army, so now we can save the world! Well, almost."

The two girls ran as fast as they could, and when they reached the tree, they realized it was a lot harder to get to the top with only two people instead of four. Kasandra told Darling to climb onto her back, and then Kasandra pushed her up into the tree. Then, Darling reached her hand down and pulled Kasandra up into the tree with her. Here, they hoped to avoid the kangaroo army. Once they were safely in the branches, Darling asked Kasandra, "How long do think we will be up here?"

Kasandra peeked through some branches. "I'm not quite sure. Maybe twenty minutes?" Darling nodded then sat down to twiddle her thumbs.

A while later, Kasandra looked down, and saw the kangaroos had only moved a couple of feet in the past ten to fifteen minutes. "Okay... so it might take a little over twenty minutes, but hey, think on the bright side. We could probably go down now and have at least an hour before they reach us."

"But the problem isn't how far away they are, it's the fact that the M.M.D. will only last a half hour, not an hour," Darling stated.

77

Clearly, she remembered more about the whole gadget talk with Miss Kalisto than Kasandra did.

"Okay. Then maybe we should climb down now," Kasandra replied to her friend, letting Darling know she was ready to jump into action. Darling nodded once more. The two got ready to descend from the tree, Kasandra going down first so that she could help Darling get down. Kasandra hopped out of the tree gracefully, and Darling grabbed onto her shoulders, and finished by plopping back down next to Kasandra with even more grace.

The two girls tip-toed and hid behind a tree as if they were secret agents, like the workers of the D.E.O. in the hit TV show *Supergirl*. Kasandra snuck from tree trunk to tree trunk with Darling by her side, until they reached the tree containing the evil chip. When Kasandra started thinking about spies, there was no stopping her imagination. "What if we replace the chip with something in equal size and weight? Just like they do in the spy movies!" Kasandra suggested.

"Oh! That makes so much sense!" exclaimed Darling.

Kasandra looked around herself. But the answer was closer than she thought. She walked around, picking up pebbles, but they all weighed more or less than the chip.

"Kitty?" Darling asked. "How large is the chip?"

Kasandra glanced at the small piece of metal resting inside the tree. Kasandra took an honest guess. "I don't know. It's about the length of a rose petal."

Darling looked deep in thought. "How much do you think it weighs, Kitty?"

"Maybe a few ounces."

"Great!" Darling pulled her hair out of the bun that rested on her head. In her hand was the most amazing thing Kasandra had seen all of this fantastic mission. It was a simple bobby pin!

"Will this work?" asked Darling, handing the hair accessory to Kasandra.

"Yes!" Kasandra replied, holding the bobby pin up in the air like Simba was held in Disney's *The Lion King*. She took a deep breath. With that, she got down on her knees, and leaned towards the tree. She worked quickly to seize the chip and toss the bobby pin in the chip's place inside the tree. Before she knew it, the tree had sealed back together and she was holding the evil chip in her hands.

"Daring Deer, we did it!" Kasandra squealed, rushing over to hug her friend. The two girls giggled and smiled, until they realized they still had a crowd of kangaroos behind them, and they weren't moving slowly anymore. Not only that, but John and Shakira remained in the center of it all.

Chapter Thirteen

Goodbye for Now

"Kasandra? Darling?" Kasandra heard a faint voice say. *Shakira!* Kasandra recognized the voice. She was about to run over to Shakira, John, and Mojo, but suddenly realized that they were still stuck inside the herd of kangaroos.

John's head popped up from the ground. "Why am I eating grass?" he asked, looking puzzled.

Shakira burst out laughing, then she gave John the "I'm sorry that just happened" look.

John glared at Shakira. Then he looked around, noticing that he was surrounded by the kangaroo army. "Oh, come on!" he exclaimed.

Kasandra looked around too, and noticed that the kangaroos no longer appeared to be possessed. They just looked like a bunch of kangaroos hopping around and munching on grass.

Phew! Everything looks back to normal, thought Kasandra. Then she saw a small opening in the circle of kangaroos that she might be able to make it through to get to John and Shakira. Kasandra patted Darling on the shoulder, then she pointed towards the gap in between two of the largest kangaroos.

Darling nodded in response, then shrugged her shoulders as if she was saying, "I can't see what you're pointing at."

"Oh, sorry. Here." Kasandra grabbed the pen out of her pocket once more and handed it to Darling. "You can aim for the kangaroos, just to the north of us, so we can slow them down. That will open the perfect space for me to grab Peacock Princess and The Parrot, then sprint back over to you," Kasandra whispered to her friend.

"Okay," Darling whispered back.

Darling got the pen ready, and Kasandra started charging towards the kangaroos. With only moments to spare, Darling fired the pen, aiming straight at the mob. The blast hit them, making them slower by the second. Kasandra ran her butt off to get to the center and grab her friends. She dodged some slow-motion jumping kangaroos, and dashed right into the center.

"Thank goodness you're okay!" She ran over to Shakira, and gave her a hug as if she would never see her again. Then she skipped over to John and paused before giving him a hug too. She stopped, and they both smiled at each other nervously.

"Okay, love bugs! Let's go over to Darling!" Shakira exclaimed, not realizing that the girls had been using code names.

Clearly, she was excited to be in the company of her Animal Guard friends once more.

When they all dodged the slow-mo kangaroos, they finally reached where Darling was standing. Shakira ran over to Darling and hugged her tightly. While this was happening, John was just to the left of them, picking grass out of his teeth. "This is disgusting! Why didn't you guys stop me?"

Kasandra laughed at John's silly statement. "Well, you happened to be possessed by this." Kasandra held up the "chip of darkness," as she and Darling nicknamed it.

Shakira stared at the small chip. "That's why we were under Crow and Vulture's control? How come you two weren't affected?"

Kasandra was about to answer her, but then she realized that Mojo wasn't with them, *again*. "I'll tell you in a sec."

Kasandra turned around and calmly walked over to the group of kangaroos once more. There was Mojo, right in the center, doing flips and cartwheels. He was trying to get as much attention as he could now that the kangaroos didn't look angry anymore.

"Mojo!" Kasandra shouted. Mojo fell down onto his bottom, then ran over to her quickly. The furry koala climbed up Kasandra's back, and like a cowboy, he threw his hands in the air and shouted, "Ye-haw!" With that, Kasandra sprinted back to her fellow Animal Guard agents. The group laughed.

Now that the commotion was over, the foursome figured they should get going. Their parents were probably worried sick. Mojo hopped off of Kasandra's back, and sat on the ground like a puppy waiting for a treat.

"Bye, buddy," said John, giving the tiny koala a fist bump. Mojo practically smiled, even though they weren't quite sure if koalas could do that. John walked away and stood by the robot tree.

Next, it was Darling's turn to say goodbye. "Thanks, Mojo. Today, I believe, you are the first animal to help save the world. I'm gonna miss you so much!" Darling told him, wiping a small tear from her eye, then giving him a large hug. She moved and stood next to John, waiting for Shakira and Kasandra to finish their goodbyes.

Shakira rushed over to Mojo and gave him a tight squeeze, then whispered in his ear, "Mojo, you are the closest thing I will probably ever have to a pet. Like ever." She laughed, then blew him a kiss before returning to her friends.

"I'm gonna miss you the most," Kasandra told him with a smile. "Hey, Mojo?"

He looked at her. "Yeah, La-sandra?" he asked, his Australian accent even stronger than before.

"I just want you to know that I will never, ever, ever, ever forget you. I love you!" She was about to hug him, but then Mojo surprised Kasandra by jumping up and hugging her first. Not the other way around. Her heart melted at the lovely moment, so she reached out and hugged him back. "Never change who you are, Mojo. I'm counting on you."

Kasandra stepped back, joining her friends. She waved goodbye one last time, then looked at her team. *This is one amazing team!* she thought. Kasandra smiled. Well, tried to smile. Then, she said sadly, "Goodbye, Australia." With that, she reached her hand into the center of the circle of friends she was bordering.

"Let's go home," Shakira said, placing her hand in the center as well.

Darling nodded, then placed her hand on top of Shakira's.

"I'm gonna miss it here." John sighed.

Kasandra glanced back at a sad-looking Mojo. "I bet we could always ask Miss Kalisto if it would be okay to visit Mojo every once in a while." Mojo smiled at the clever idea.

They gave one final wave goodbye before John gently rested his hand on top of the pile. Once his palm touched the others, their rings lit up, and Kasandra and her fellow agents disappeared into thin air.

Mojo smiled. "I'm gonna miss ya, girlie." He turned and wandered back towards his tree.

Chapter Fourteen

Got Away Again

Kasandra laughed with her friends as they reappeared in the dusty attic of her house. She looked around. All of her friends were standing there, all smiling. Then, John plugged in the long gray cord that connected the computer to the wall. Miss Kalisto's sort-of-smiling face came into view on the pixelated computer screen. When her smile faded, her eyebrows rose and she directed her gaze at Kasandra.

"Oh!" Kasandra said, realizing why Miss Kalisto was glaring at her. "Here." She held up the small chip and slowly approached the screen.

"Thank you, Agent Cortez."

Kasandra nodded. She watched as the chip vanished from her fingers. Only seconds later, it was in Miss Kalisto's hands. Studying the tiny item, Miss Kalisto continued speaking. "This will be going to a high security area where we can study it more."

"Well, that sounds protected," Shakira mumbled.

"As for Crow and Vulture," Miss Kalisto continued.

Kasandra quickly cut her off, with great disappointment in her voice. "I know. We let them get away. Again."

"Agent Cortez, here at the Animal Guard we do not expect our younger agents to stop criminals that we have been after for years. However, you did help us track them."

"How?" Kasandra asked with surprise.

Miss Kalisto took a breath and began to explain. "Your agent trackers told us where you were at all times during the mission. This information will allow us to begin to track down Crow and Vulture."

Darling's head lifted up. "You mean we really just helped save the world? Even from Crow and Vulture? Well, maybe not completely, but sort of?"

"Yes, Agent Adams. You helped save the world, but not all of it. You saved some of it. You helped us here at the Animal Guard greatly on our hunt for Crow and Vulture," Miss Kalisto said with pride.

Just hearing her say these words made Kasandra feel happy. She was thrilled at the idea of being a hero for the kangaroos of Australia. It just sounded so exciting. So fun. So adventurous!

Miss Kalisto gave the team a smile (it was almost a complete smile this time!). Before leaving them she said, "Congratulations once again, agents."

With that, John unplugged the wire, before quickly plugging it back in again. Miss Kalisto appeared on the screen once more. She looked rather confused, wondering why the youngsters wanted to talk again.

"One last thing," John said. "Can you maybe send the three of us home? Ya know, with that poof-disappear thing? Please?" John was worried that his parents might scold him for not being at the dinner table.

"Well," Miss Kalisto replied. "I don't see why not."

"Yes!" Shakira cheered, jumping up in the air with her arms spread wide.

With a flick of Miss Kalisto's wrist, John, Darling, and Shakira disappeared. Kasandra smiled, shut off the computer, and began to wonder what her own parents might be thinking: *Where is their daughter? Is Kasandra safe? Who is she with?* There were billions of possible questions she would soon need to answer.

Better get it over with... Kasandra told herself. She carefully worked her way out of the attic. She climbed down the spiral staircase and opened the dark wooden door. She rushed through the hallway and down the stairs to the kitchen. There, Kasandra found her father laying his hand on her mother's back. Mom's head was buried in her hands. It looked like she was crying.

"Mom? Dad?" asked Kasandra, as she moved closer to her panic-stricken parents.

"My goodness!" Her mother jumped up and ran over to hug her youngest daughter. Dad rushed over to Kasandra too and let out a huge sigh of relief. He hugged Kasandra and asked, "Where were you, sweets?"

Kasandra took a deep breath. "It doesn't matter."

"Why, honey? We were worried sick!" her mother exclaimed.

Kasandra felt the light drop of a bottle in her pocket. *The amnesia spray!* Almost immediately, she pulled out the spray and held it behind her back.

"Well, you see, it won't matter because you won't remember that any of this even happened," she told her parents. They looked puzzled. Kasandra pulled out the spray from behind her back, and then glanced at the clock. *5:30. Great! This means I should spray them twice to cover the two hours that I was gone.*

Kasandra held up the bottle and aimed the spray in the direction of her parents. Then, she gently pressed down two times, covering them in a silvery mist.

Mom closed her eyes for a moment. When she opened them, she said, "Kasandra, sweetie?"

"Yes, Mommy?"

"Did you finish your homework?"

"Mmhmm."

Mom glanced at the stove. "Well, I should get dinner ready. We're having cranberry chili tonight!" With that, Mom walked over to the fridge and pulled out a container of fresh cranberries.

Kasandra smiled. Everything was back to the way it was before today's Animal Guard excursions. She leaned over and kissed her father on the cheek before going upstairs to her room.

Kasandra started to step into her bedroom, but then moved back out towards the hallway. She walked into Maria's room, only to find her sister stretched out on the bed. "Can I use the phone?" she asked cheerily, plopping down onto the bed next to Maria.

"Sure, Kitty." Maria pointed to her desk. Kasandra walked over to the desk and grabbed the phone. She was about to leave the room when Maria questioned, "Why are you so happy today?"

Kasandra thought for a moment. "It was just a nice day, I guess." She shrugged, then walked out of the room. She began to type in the digits of Shakira's number when she heard Mom call her down to the kitchen to help prepare dinner.

Chapter Fifteen

A Day of Surprises

It was the first game of the soccer season and Kasandra was beyond excited. She slipped on blue shorts and her new team jersey. The jersey was very soft and light. To represent the MaryEllen Bay Middle school colors, the shirt was blue, and at the top of the shoulder blades, it had white lines that ran down to the edge of the short sleeves. On the front was a small patch with the letters MBMS on it with a soccer ball underneath. The back was Kasandra's favorite part of her jersey, the part that showed who she was on the team. Her last name was written in big white letters, spelling "CORTEZ," just above the large white number "10." Kasandra was especially proud of this number because it was the same jersey number that all-star soccer player, Pelé (from Brazil!), once wore.

Kasandra rushed into the bathroom, grabbed a hair tie, and pulled her long locks up into a ponytail. The ponytail reached her shoulders and allowed lots of bouncy curls to cascade over her head.

90

She slipped on shoes, remembering that she still needed her soccer bag which contained her other pieces of equipment.

I have to be at the school in 10-15 minutes, so I might as well put on my cleats when I get to MBMS, Kasandra decided before running back to her room to grab the Nike bag off of the floor under her bed. She zoomed downstairs, fast enough that Mom would have yelled at her if she saw her. Once she was in the kitchen, Kasandra quickly picked up the full blue-and-white water bottle that the school had provided for her. (Everything else, besides the uniform and water bottle, she had to purchase with Mom and Dad!)

Kasandra ran out the front door and hopped into Dad's car. "We thought you got lost!" Dad exclaimed from the driver's seat. Kasandra laughed. She saw her mom in the passenger seat and Maria to her left. She smiled as Dad began to pull away from the house.

Once they arrived at MaryEllen Bay Middle School, Dad pulled in through the bus loop, allowing Kasandra to jump out so she could go join up with her team. Mom leaned out of the window to kiss Kasandra before Dad pulled away to find them a place to park.

As the rest of her family drove off into the rectangular parking lot, Kasandra walked inside and headed to her locker. She planned to meet Darling, Shakira, and John there before the game. She walked up to her locker to find only John and Shakira standing there. Before she had the chance to ask where on Earth Darling was, Shakira blurted, "She had to go take care of something."

Kasandra nodded, then sat on the ground below her locker to slip on her blue and white game socks and shin guards. Next, she put on her pink cleats with the phrase "Live Free" printed in Portuguese on the side. At that moment, she realized that the ponytail holder in her hair matched the glittery pink laces of her cleats. She smiled at the thought of it, then shoved the bag into her crammed locker, just after taking out her water bottle.

"Okay. Let's go!" Kasandra exclaimed, slamming the locker door shut. The three laughed at how loud the slamming of her locker door was.

Kasandra led the way out to the soccer field behind the school building. The sidelines were crowded. And when I say crowded, I mean it was *crowded*. Tons of people, both young and old, were sitting in the stands along the field. Kasandra saw the opposing team, the Ruster Academy Roosters, passing the ball back and forth on one half of the field, already warming up for the game.

At the front row of the bleachers was the cheer squad, except Kasandra noticed that two girls were missing. And she knew exactly who those girls were. "I'll be right back," she told John and Shakira.

"Okay. We'll go tell Coach that you're here," John replied.

Kasandra nodded once more, and walked across the field to find Darling talking to Jessica under a nearby tree. Not arguing, but actually *talking*. Darling then walked away, leaving Jessica with a large smirk pasted on her face. Darling approached Kasandra, and

Kasandra could tell that whatever the "chat" was that they just had, Darling didn't come out victorious.

"What's goin' on?" she asked Darling.

"I worked so hard and now I can't have the job!" Darling sulked.

"What do you mean?"

"I mean.... since I'm going to be gone for a few weeks for my guide dog training, I can't be cheer captain anymore. And of course, Principal Morrison insists that Jessica take my place, starting today. And trust me, talking to Jessica is like making a deal with the devil!" Darling complained.

"Wow. That's terrible. Are you still on the team?" asked Kasandra, immediately feeling terrible for her friend.

"Yeah, but only until I leave, which is, um, yeah... this Saturday," Darling replied with a frown.

Kasandra could see that Darling was miserable and she felt she had to do something for her. So she leaned in and hugged Darling tightly. "I promise we can talk about it some more after the game," she said softly.

Darling sighed. "Thanks for being such a good friend."

Kasandra smiled, then hugged her friend again before rushing over to her soccer team. Coach Jim looked at her, then began to go over game plays and strategies.

But Kasandra just couldn't hear it all. Even with the bad news from Darling, Kasandra still had so many positive thoughts racing through her mind, easily outrunning the negative ones. Darling may be feeling down right now, but in the next hour or so, Kasandra knew Darling would be feeling better again. The group of friends were throwing a surprise "going away" party for Darling after the soccer game. They had been planning the party since they returned from their crazy kangaroo mission a few weeks ago. She knew that soon everyone would be joyful. After all, they were going to have ice cream and Mom's famous chocolate lava cake!

Kasandra took in her surroundings and grinned. Everything was fabulous at the Animal Guard, even though the missions were often unexpected. Her life was great. The Animal Guard was great. Her soccer team was great. Her family was great. But most importantly, Kasandra's group of friends was great!